P9-DED-828

GREENWILLOW BOOKS, New York

The photographs were reproduced from 35-mm slides
and printed in full color.

Copyright © 1987 by Tana Hoban. All rights reserved. No part
of this book may be reproduced or utilized in any form or by
any means, electronic or mechanical including photo-
copying, recording or by any information storage and retrieval
system, without permission in writing from the Publisher,
Greenwillow Books, a division of William Morrow &
Company, Inc., 105 Madison Avenue, New York, N.Y. 10016.
Printed in Singapore by Tien Wah
First Edition 10 9 8 7 6 5 4 3 2 1

Library of Congress Cataloging-in-Publication Data
Hoban, Tana. Dots, spots, speckles, and stripes.
Summary: Photographs show dots, spots, speckles, and stripes as
found on clothing, flowers, faces, animals, and other places.
1. Form perception—Juvenile literature.
[1. Shape. 2. Form perception] I. Title.
BF293.H62 1987 152.1′423 86-22919
ISBN 0-688-06862-6 ISBN 0-688-06863-4 (lib. bdg.)

For Miela and Bob,
Max and Jen
—where this book began

52.1
Hel
9189

150
150
150
200
80
130

T BY AIR
32-0600
61-4665
TOYOTA

CRYSTAL LAKE SCHOOL LIBRARY